K'TONTON IN THE CIRCUS

Other Books by the Author

What Danny Did
What the Moon Brought
The Singing Way: A Book of Verse for the Jewish Child
Little New Angel
Molly and the Sabbath Queen
Our Baby: A Record Book for the Jewish Child
Jewish Heroes
Dick, the Horse That Kept the Sabbath
Ten and a Kid

K'TONTON BOOKS

The Adventures of K'tonton
K'tonton in Israel
K'tonton on an Island in the Sea
The Best of K'tonton

SADIE ROSE
WEILERSTEIN

ILLUSTRATED BY
MARILYN HIRSH

PHILADELPHIA 5742/1981
THE JEWISH PUBLICATION SOCIETY OF AMERICA

K'TONTON

IN THE

CIRCUS

A HANUKKAH

ADVENTURE

© *1981 by Sadie Rose Weilerstein*
Illustrations © 1981 by Marilyn Hirsh
All rights reserved   First paperback edition
Manufactured in the United States of America

Library of Congress Cataloging in Publication Data
Weilerstein, Sadie Rose, 1894–
K'tonton in the circus.
Summary: The adventures of a thumb-sized Jewish boy
who joins the circus by mistake and celebrates Hanukkah with his circus friends.
[1. Jewish—Fiction. 2. Hanukkah—Fiction.
3. Circus stories] I. Hirsh, Marilyn, ill. II. Title.
PZ7.W435Ks   [Fic]   81-11765
ISBN 0-8276-0196-4   AACR2

Designed by Adrianne Onderdonk Dudden

To
Elizabeth and Rachel Dena
who read this story in manuscript
and to
Adam and Joseph
Debra
Nomi and Daniel
who I hope will read it someday

CONTENTS

K'TONTON IN THE CIRCUS

INTRODUCING K'TONTON

This is K'tonton, a tiny Jewish boy no bigger than a thumb. Like other thumblings, he was born in answer to his mother's prayer. "Oh, that I might have a child," she prayed. "I should not mind if he were no bigger than a thumb."

When K'tonton was eight days old, his parents named him Isaac Samuel. They said, "God has heard our prayers. Now there is joy and laughter in our home. Our son shall be called Isaac, which means 'laughter,' and Samuel, which means 'God heard.' But for everyday they called him K'tonton—from the Hebrew *katan*, "small," *k'tonton*, "very small."

K'tonton's mother added honey from the Land of Israel to the baby's milk. She sang him Hebrew lullabies. His father taught him Torah.

By the time K'tonton was three years old, he repeated Bible verses the way other children recite nursery rhymes.

He also asked endless questions, climbed and swung on things, and got in and out of mischief. At the age of four, he had his first adventure.

K'tonton has grown since then. He is now fully four inches tall. And he has gone on having adventures: at home in Brooklyn, on an island in the sea, in the circus, and in Israel. Although his adventures in the circus happened before he went to Israel, this is the first account of them in print.

> K'tonton's official biographer,
> Sadie Rose Weilerstein

K'TONTON MAKES A MISTAKE

It was a mistake that got tiny, thumb-sized K'tonton into a circus. K'tonton made the mistake when his parents brought him to a small town in South Carolina to visit an aunt.

In Brooklyn, where K'tonton lived, the days were growing cold, but in South Carolina it was still warm. K'tonton sat under a fig tree in his aunt's backyard, looking at a grapevine that grew nearby. The fig tree and the vine reminded him of a verse in the Bible: "In that day . . . they shall sit, every one under his vine and under his fig tree. And none shall make them afraid." Why wouldn't they be afraid? Because "in that day" there would be no more wars. All the people in the world would be friends. The Bible says so. "Nations shall beat their swords into plowshares and their spears into pruning hooks."

K'tonton was sure they would do it to the guns and

tanks too. They probably would turn them into farm trac-
tors or combines. It would all begin in Jerusalem in the time
of the *Mashiach*, the Messiah. And this set K'tonton thinking about the Prophet Elijah. Someday the good prophet
would come to tell them it was happening. He might appear
at the close of the Sabbath when they sing, "Elijah the
Prophet, come soon, soon," or on Passover night when they
open the door for him. It could be any day.

K'tonton thought about Elijah when he lay in his little
bed that night. He thought of him the next morning when
his father tucked him into his pocket and carried him to the
synagogue. It was the first day of Kislev, the Hebrew month
in which Hanukkah begins. K'tonton was still thinking
about Elijah when the services were over and his father set
him down on a sunny windowsill.

"Wait here for me, K'tonton," his father said. "I want
to talk to the rabbi. Stay right where you are."

But K'tonton didn't stay where his father had left him.
The day was warm, and the window was open.

"I may as well wait in the fresh air," K'tonton thought,
and he walked through the open window to the ledge outside.

There he stood, singing softly to himself. K'tonton
often did this when he was alone. He sang "*Am Yisrael Hai
—The People of Israel Live On.*" He sang "*Sim Shalom—
Send Peace.*"

He was singing "Elijah the Prophet, Elijah the Tish-
bite, Elijah of Gilead, come soon, soon," when the sound of
a trumpet made him look up. A tall, bearded man on a white
horse was riding by. He wore a long robe and a turban and

held a silver trumpet in his hand. A banner attached to his saddle advertised a circus, but K'tonton was too excited to notice this.

"Elijah, Elijah!" K'tonton cried out. "You've come! *Baruch haba!* Welcome in the name of the Lord!" And he bowed solemnly.

The man turned. For a moment he looked as surprised as K'tonton. Then he rode right onto the sidewalk. He picked K'tonton up, tucked him into his sash, and rode away.

For a while K'tonton was too dazed to lift his head above the sash. When he did, they had turned down a country road. In the distance he saw tents with flying banners.

"Jerusalem!" K'tonton thought joyfully. "Elijah has brought me to Jerusalem!" But of course it wasn't Jerusalem. It was a circus, a small, one-ring, tent circus that traveled from town to town throughout the South.

Inside the gates, the rider dismounted in front of a small tent and went inside. A stout man was sitting there smoking a big cigar. His feet were up on a desk.

The rider pulled K'tonton out of his sash and set him down on the desk. "Look what I picked up," he said. "He'll be a bigger sensation than that human cannonball we once had."

The circus master's feet came down. He stared at the tiny person in front of him.

"He's real," he said at last. "A genuine, real live thumb-sized boy. Not even General Tom Thumb was as small as this. Have you got a name?" he asked K'tonton.

"Of course," K'tonton answered. "Everyone has a name. I'm K'tonton ben Baruch Reuben."

"Good! K'tonton will be enough. I'll put you in the Tent of the World's Wonders."

K'tonton looked around for the rider, but he was no longer there.

The circus master picked up K'tonton and left the tent.

THE SIDESHOW

The Tent of the World's Wonders, to which K'tonton was taken, was on the midway. This was a part of the circus that people visited before and after the performance. It was like a carnival. K'tonton was carried past food stands, a souvenir booth, and a small zoo to a tent called a sideshow. Here he was put on exhibition between the Fat Lady and the Human Skeleton.

The Wild Man of Borneo and the Sword Swallower were also in the tent. Later, when K'tonton came to know the Sword Swallower better, he tried to get him to beat his sword into a plow. But the Sword Swallower said if he did he'd lose his job. Besides, he didn't use his sword to fight with, just to entertain people.

Outside, the barker shouted, "This way, folks! Only two dimes and a nickel to see the World's Wonders, including K'tonton, the smallest person on earth. He's four inches tall. That's right, just ten centimeters from head to toe!

Measure him yourself, folks. Your money back if he is one centimeter taller."

Inside the tent, the Wild Man of Borneo shook the bars of his cage and roared, and the Sword Swallower swallowed swords and sharp knives. Visitors hardly noticed them. They crowded around K'tonton's stand, gaping in wonder. Every few minutes, K'tonton got up to be measured. Then the guard sold pictures of him standing against a wooden ruler.

"Get your picture here, folks," the guard called. "Amaze the folks at home. One dime for a picture autographed by the little fellow himself."

Then K'tonton sat down in a doll-sized chair before a doll-sized table and wrote his name on the pictures in thin, spidery letters.

Mind you, K'tonton didn't like being an exhibit. It made him unhappy to have people pay admission to stare at him because he was so small. K'tonton's size was what he liked least about himself. He was always hoping that someday he would wake up to find himself regular-sized, like his friends. Nor did K'tonton like to hear people say right in front of him, "How tiny! Do you suppose he's real?" He didn't even like autographing his pictures.

"I wouldn't mind it if I were a great scholar and had written an important book," K'tonton thought, "but . . ."

A child's voice made him look up. A little boy was pulling at his mother's sleeve with one hand and pointing at K'tonton with the other.

"I want him. Buy him for me, Mommy. Buy him!"

K'tonton wanted to scream, "I'm not a plaything. I'm

a person!" Instead he pressed so hard against his tiny pencil that it left a hole in the picture he was autographing.

"I'm nothing but a freak," K'tonton told himself after the boy and his mother moved on, "and now I have to live with freaks." K'tonton looked at the fat lady crowded into her oversized chair. He looked at her three chins, her bulging arms, and turned away.

A gentle voice made him look back. The voice reminded him of his mother. K'tonton was surprised to see it was the Fat Lady who was talking to him.

"Don't you feel well, dearie? Can I help you?" Kind eyes looked down at him.

Another Bible verse came into K'tonton's head: " 'Man looks at the outward appearance, but the Lord looks into the heart.' Maybe she's different only on the outside, not the inside," K'tonton thought.

For the first time since he had been brought into the tent, K'tonton smiled. The Fat Lady smiled back.

Late that afternoon two boys stopped before K'tonton's stand. "Watch me make that little guy squeal," the taller one said with a mean grin. The next minute K'tonton saw a pin coming toward him. He was too frightened to move. The pin pierced his jacket and touch his skin, but it went no farther. The Human Skeleton pushed it away. His bony fist sent the boy sprawling.

"Try that again and I'll squash you like a bug," the Fat Lady yelled at the boys as they made for the door.

K'tonton wanted to thank his neighbors for their kindness.

"Thank you, Miss—Miss—," he began. Then he stopped. He didn't know what to call her. He couldn't say, "Miss Fat Lady."

The Fat Lady understood. "Call me Daisy," she said. "That's my name. All my friends call me Daisy."

"And I'm John," the Human Skeleton said.

K'tonton knew that he had friends in the circus.

Night came. The last show was over. The tents were coming down. Papa Joe, the man who supervised the setting up and taking down of the circus, looked at K'tonton and scratched his head.

"It don't pay to be reliable," he said to Daisy and John.

"The boss says to me, 'That new tent rigger quit. I want you to take over. You've filled in before. I'm depending on you.'"

"I tell him, 'I'm a performer, not a tent rigger.' He says, 'You can do both jobs.' Today he brings me the little one. 'Look at this new find we got hold of,' he says to me. 'Set him up and keep a sharp eye on him.' So now I've got three jobs! What am I supposed to do with the little one? I can't let him sleep in the big trailer truck. It's no place for a child."

"I would take him to my camper," Daisy said, "but I can hardly squeeze in myself." She laughed. "There wouldn't be much left of him if I rolled over in the night."

"Why can't we take him to our own camper, Papa?"

A young girl had come in, Papa Joe's little daughter Lillibelle. Her eyes were lavender blue, and her golden curls were tied back with a bow. To K'tonton, listening anxiously to all the talk, she seemed like an angel. Any minute she might fly away. The truth was that Lillibelle *could* fly—on a trapeze. Her mother, billed as "La Belle, World Famous Aerialist," was teaching her.

"Why can't we take him? Please, Papa!"

"Because you, your mama, and me are in the camper already. And there's the chihuahua your mama has and that monkey you were set on keeping." Papa Joe looked at K'tonton again. "Still, he wouldn't take up much space. I'll tell you what. You ask your mama. If she says 'yes,' I say 'yes.'"

So K'tonton went home with Lillibelle. The camper was neat and homey inside. Starched white curtains were tied back at the windows. A little chihuahua jumped on Lillibelle, barking and licking her hand. Just one hand!

Lillibelle's other hand was holding K'tonton. And hanging by one arm from a curtain rod was a small monkey. He was looking down at K'tonton.

"His name is George," Lillibelle said. "I named him after a monkey in a book. The dog's name is Chichi."

Mama Belle was sewing spangles on a dress. "So this is the little one," she said. "But of course he shall stay. Tonight you sleep in your clothing," she told K'tonton. "Tomorrow I will make you pajamas."

"Daisy and John are my friends," K'tonton thought to himself, "and as long as I'm here Lillibelle, Mama Belle, and Papa Joe will be my family."

NEW WORDS, NEW FRIENDS, AND SOMETHING TO EAT

It is hard to give up a beautiful dream. Even when K'tonton knew he was in the circus, he still believed that the man on the white horse was Elijah. Perhaps he believed it because he so much wanted it to be true.

"Maybe this is just a stopping place," he told himself. "Probably he has gone to bring my father and mother. They'll be here any day now."

No one asked K'tonton about his parents. Boys often ran away to the circus. Workers—called roustabouts—came and went. If they didn't say where they had come from, no one asked.

But Lillibelle wondered about K'tonton. Did he have a family? Did he have a brother like Tom Thumb or a little sister like Thumbelina? Had he been born in some strange way, like the tiny Peachstone Boy of Japan, who came out of a peach? Maybe his parents were too poor to keep him, like in "Hansel and Gretel," and he didn't want to talk about it.

Lillibelle was too polite to ask K'tonton these personal questions, but she was glad to answer his.

There was so much in the circus K'tonton had to get used to. It was strange to go to bed in one town and wake up in another. It was strange and exciting to see the tents taken down each night and set up again in the morning. Trucks unloaded tent poles, canvas, wire, lumber for seats. Animal cages on gaily painted wagons rolled off the flat cars.

There were circus terms K'tonton had to learn. Here are a few of them:

BIG TOP: the main tent where the performance takes place. The one in K'tonton's circus was so round and big, it had to be put together with stakes, center poles, side poles, metal rings, rope, and many yards of canvas. Tent riggers, canvasmen, and Jumbo the elephant set it up.

ARENA: the inside of the big top.

RING: the raised circle in the middle of the arena where the acts are staged. Some circuses have three rings. K'tonton's had only one.

SPECTACLE: the grand parade inside the arena that begins the performance. Performers in sparkling costumes—acrobats, aerialists, bareback riders on prancing horses, tightrope walkers—circle the arena. Clowns run in and out, making people laugh.

SIDESHOW: the tent where K'tonton was an exhibit. It is open only before and after the performance in the Big Top.

COOKHOUSE: the tent where the circus people eat.

There were more new people for K'tonton to meet. Three became K'tonton's special friends: the flapjack man, Tomas the animal trainer, and Clarence, a clown.

The flapjack man made pancakes on a griddle. K'tonton liked to watch him flip a pancake over, toss it into the air, and catch it on a pancake turner like a juggler.

Tomas looked after the animals. The circus wasn't a large one. It had only one elephant, a trained seal in a portable pool, three palomino horses, six performing dogs, a dancing bear, and a lion. The lion was very old and no longer performed. He was kept in the small zoo on the midway. Most of his teeth were gone and his mane was dull, but he still could roar and look fierce.

Along with Lillibelle, Clarence became one of K'tonton's best friends. Clarence taught him clown tricks and the many ways he made people laugh. And he introduced him to the other clowns. One of them was Skyhigh.

The first time K'tonton saw Skyhigh, he was walking into the arena. He was so tall that K'tonton was sure he was a giant, maybe one of the *Anakim* the Bible tells about. But then Clarence explained that Skyhigh wasn't tall at all.

"He is walking on stilts," Clarence said. "You can't see them because he wears them under his pants. It's the stilts that make him look so tall."

A thought came to K'tonton: "If I had stilts, I would be twice as tall."

And the next day K'tonton did have stilts. Clarence surprised him with a pair that were just the right size for a thumb-sized boy. K'tonton looked pleased and proud as he practiced walking on them. If he had to be thumb-sized, it was nice to be the size of a giant's thumb.

With so much to see and learn and wonder about, there were days when K'tonton hardly missed his father and mother—except at mealtime. That was because he was careful not to eat any food that wasn't kosher. Every time he sat down to a meal he remembered his own home, where he could eat everything.

"All you take is cereal and milk and a bit of salad," Daisy said to him one day. "Are you a vegetarian?"

K'tonton didn't know what a vegetarian was, but he was sure he wasn't one.

"I'm Jewish. I eat only kosher," he said. And he told her about the foods he never ate: shellfish, pork, and bacon, and about other foods he ate but only if they were prepared in a special way.

Daisy was glad her diet wasn't like K'tonton's. "But it's his religion," she explained to the others. "We have to help him."

She bought him a little salt dish to use as a plate, a tiny

silver spoon to go with it, and a small-sized thimble for his milk.

"It's all right for you to eat the bread," she assured him. "Cook says it's made with pure vegetable shortening."

Mama Belle made him tasty fruit and vegetable salads. The popcorn man sent him a whole kernel of popcorn every day. One kernel was more than enough for three meals. In the cookhouse, where the circus people ate, Lillibelle always urged K'tonton to take a bit of her baked potato or hard-boiled egg or tuna fish. "You can use your own spoon," she would say.

K'tonton wished his mother could see all the good kosher food his friends brought him. She always worried that he didn't eat enough.

A BOY IN THE LION'S CAGE

On one of K'tonton's first days in the circus, there was a commotion on the midway. Later K'tonton learned that he himself had been the cause of the commotion, although he knew nothing about it at the time.

The morning began quietly. Lillibelle was in the camper doing her homework. She didn't go to school, so her lessons were sent to her by mail. George, the little monkey, looked over her shoulder, pretending to read. K'tonton didn't have to pretend. He could read Hebrew from right to left and English from left to right. Now he sat cross-legged on the table trying to read Lillibelle's lesson book upside down.

After a while Lillibelle looked up at the clock. "K'tonton," she said, "it's time for you to leave for the exhibit. Do you think you can go by yourself? I have to finish my schoolwork."

The camper was parked behind the sideshow, so there wasn't far to go.

"Of course I can go by myself," K'tonton answered. "I'm small but I'm not a baby."

Lillibelle didn't have to get up to let him out. Papa Joe had cut a small opening in the bottom of the door, just big enough for a thumb-sized person to get through. He wanted to make sure that K'tonton could get into the camper even when the family wasn't there. A rope led to the ground. K'tonton took hold of the rope and slid down.

"Go straight to the tent," Lillibelle called after him.

K'tonton meant to do as Lillibelle said, but there was so much in the midway he wanted to see. K'tonton's curiosity was bigger than he was.

"It's early," he told himself. "The gates aren't even open. I'll look around a little and then go back. There's plenty of time." And K'tonton walked away from the sideshow instead of toward it. By the time the commotion began, he had returned to the tent and was sitting in his place between Daisy and John.

This is how the trouble started. A kindergarten teacher had brought her class to the circus. "The children can't wait to see the lion," the teacher said to the P.T.A. mother who was helping her. She pointed to the boys and girls hurrying toward the animal cages.

"Miss Roberts!" A solemn-eyed boy looked up at the teacher. He had been leaning against the rope that kept visitors from getting too close to the cage. "Miss Roberts, I saw a boy in the cage!"

Miss Roberts quickly counted the children. "You must have imagined it, Jimmy," she said. "We're all here, and there's no boy in the cage."

"He *was* in the cage," Jimmy insisted. "I saw him."

"Maybe he saw the keeper," the P.T.A. mother suggested. But Jimmy said it wasn't a man. It was a boy!

The children were all listening.

"Jimmy, you must not make up stories," the teacher said. She was losing her patience. "If a boy was in the cage, where is he now?"

Jimmy didn't answer. He was almost in tears at not being believed. A chubby, freckle-faced little girl answered for him. "Maybe the lion ate the boy up," she suggested. "Maybe it chewed him all up and swallowed him down."

At that moment the lion, who had been half asleep, opened his mouth wide and roared. Some of the children screamed. One turned and began to run. The teacher was trying to calm him when Papa Joe hurried over.

"What's this about a lion eating up a boy?" he asked. "That lion wouldn't hurt you even if you stuck your head in his mouth."

"Look," he said, "the door is locked tight. How could a boy get in?"

"He walked through the bars," Jimmy said. "He was very small."

"A small boy, you say. How small?"

Jimmy held his fingers a few inches apart.

"Relax, folks," Papa Joe smiled. "The mystery is solved. What Jimmy saw was our latest exhibit, K'tonton, the smallest living person in the world. Let me lead you to him. There'll be no admission charge," he assured the teacher.

A crowd followed them to the sideshow.

"Our guests!" Papa Joe said to the barker as he waved the children in. "Only the kindergarten class," he added as the crowd surged forward. "The rest of you stop here," and he pointed to the ticket booth.

"K'tonton," Papa Joe asked, "did you visit the lion this morning?"

K'tonton nodded.

"I thought so. You gave these children an awful scare. They thought the lion had eaten you up. Shake hands with them so they'll see you're all here."

Each boy and girl got a handshake, or rather a pinky shake. The child held out a little finger, and K'tonton shook it with both his hands. Then K'tonton autographed one of his pictures for them to hang up in the classroom.

"K'tonton," Papa Joe said after everyone had left, "I'm not going to scold you, but you must never, never walk into a cage again." His voice was stern. "Even the keeper has to be careful with an animal that was once wild. As the saying goes, 'Once a wild animal, always a wild animal.' "

"But Papa Joe," K'tonton said earnestly, "the Bible says when the *Mashiach*, the Messiah, comes the animals won't be wild anymore. A lamb won't be afraid to lie down near a lion or a leopard or a bear."

"You win," said Papa Joe. "We'll compromise. When the Messiah comes you can walk into any cage you want to. But not until then! Promise me!"

K'tonton promised. But to himself he thought, "I guess Papa Joe doesn't know that the *Mashiach* is almost here. He doesn't know that Elijah is coming to take us to him."

THE STRIKE

It was Friday afternoon before K'tonton saw the man with the cigar again. The circus people called him the Big Boss.

"I knew that thumbkin would wow them," he said as he pushed through the crowd waiting for K'tonton's autograph.

"How does it feel to be a world's wonder?" he asked when K'tonton looked up. K'tonton didn't answer. Instead he told the boss very politely that he won't be working that night or the next day.

"What do you mean, you won't be working?"

"On account of the Sabbath," K'tonton explained. "The Bible says we must work six days and rest on the seventh day."

"In the circus we work *every* day," the Big Boss growled. "You stay right here on the job! Not another squeak out of you!" And he left.

Daisy's chins trembled with indignation. "The precious lamb," she exclaimed. She always called K'tonton Precious Lamb or Dearie. "The Big Boss should let K'tonton keep his Sabbath."

"Yea," John said, "but there's nothing we can do."

"Oh, yes there is," Daisy told him. "I'll go on strike." Then she got out of her seat, all four hundred ten pounds of her, and walked toward the door.

"Wait!" John called. "I'll go with you."

They started down the midway together. People turned and stared. They were a strange looking couple, the Fat Lady and the Human Skeleton.

The Big Boss was furious when they walked into his

tent. "What in blue blazes do you think you're doing?" he shouted. "Why aren't you two where you belong?"

"We've come to tell you," Daisy said, "that you must let the Little One keep his Sabbath."

"And if I don't?" the Big Boss asked angrily.

"Then you won't have a Fat Lady in your circus. I'll go on a hunger strike. I'll lose weight, pounds and pounds."

"You won't have a Thin Man either," said the Human Skeleton. "I'll start eating every fattening food I can think of: griddle cakes with butter and syrup, hot chocolate with whipped cream, oatmeal, mashed potatoes, dumplings, doughnuts, and coffee with sugar—lots of sugar."

"That's enough from you," the Boss interrupted.

But the Human Skeleton was enjoying himself. He had never liked his strict diet.

"I forgot the snacks," he went on. "I'll eat jam and bread, banana splits, marshmallow sundaes . . ."

"K'tonton has a lot of friends in the circus," said the Fat Lady. "We'll *all* go on strike."

The Big Boss looked ready to scream, but he didn't. He controlled himself. "My good people," he said. "You have misunderstood me. It is not my way to interfere with a person's religion. Tell your little friend he has my permission to keep his Sabbath." Then he yelled, "Now get back to your tent before the whole midway gets a free show!"

Daisy didn't need to be urged. "The sun is going down," she said anxiously. "K'tonton said his Sabbath begins at sundown." She hurried back to the sideshow.

"Dearie," Daisy called as she squeezed through the rear door of the tent. "The Big Boss says . . ."

But K'tonton's seat was empty. He hadn't waited for permission.

From Mama Belle's camper came his sweet, high voice, singing a welcome song to the Sabbath.

K'TONTON LEARNS MORE ABOUT THE ANIMALS

Each day K'tonton learned something new about the animals. He learned that the Snake Charmer bathed her snake in milk to make its skin shiny; that dancing horses didn't keep time to the music, but the band master kept time with them; and that a good place to pet an elephant is behind its ears.

Jumbo the elephant often picked up K'tonton with his trunk and swung him back and forth. "More!" K'tonton would call. "More!" He loved swinging. Then the elephant would curl back his trunk and set K'tonton down on his head, and K'tonton would pet him behind his floppy ears.

K'tonton also learned that Jumbo had as many jobs as Papa Joe. He helped put up the Big Top and take it down. The tent riggers couldn't have managed the tall center poles without him. He paraded in the spectacle, all spruced up, carrying a gaily covered seat, a howdah, on his back. Sometimes Lillibelle rode in it. Out in the back lot, Jumbo let children feed him peanuts. Besides the peanuts, Jumbo ate a hundred pounds of hay and twenty pounds of grain every day, and he drank thirty gallons of water. K'tonton learned all this from Tomas.

"How much water does a camel drink?" K'tonton asked. The circus didn't have a camel, but K'tonton wanted to know.

"No water when he's crossing the desert," Tomas said. "A camel can travel three or four days without water. Once he gets to a well, he'll drink six or seven gallons, maybe more!"

"Did you ever take care of a camel?" K'tonton asked.

"Not me!" said Tomas. "Camels are mean critters. Kick and bite. Always sticking their noses in the air. I can't figure out what they're so proud about. They smell terrible!"

K'tonton knew why camels were so proud. Didn't it say in the Bible that Rebecca drew water for the camels of Abraham's servant, Eliezer? Wasn't it a camel she rode on when she went to Canaan with Eliezer to become Isaac's wife? K'tonton did some quick figuring. He was good at numbers. A camel drank at least six gallons of water. Eliezer, Abraham's servant, had ten camels. Six times ten equals sixty. Rebekah must have drawn sixty gallons of water from the well, maybe more. And sixty gallons are almost two hundred forty liters. Rebekah was even kinder than K'tonton had thought.

Next to Jumbo, K'tonton was most interested in Sylvia

Seal. Her circus name was Sylvia, but Tomas called her Baby. Tomas would hold K'tonton up beside the pool and let him feed her herring. K'tonton didn't throw her whole fish like Tomas, or even big pieces, just tiny bits. But Sylvia jumped for them anyway.

"She likes you," said Tomas.

One day they were sitting beside the pool when Tomas said to K'tonton, "Maybe you've wondered how a circus this small comes to have a seal."

K'tonton hadn't wondered. This was the only circus

and the only seal he had ever known. But he didn't interrupt. K'tonton was a good listener.

"Baby's been with me since she was a newborn pup," Tomas went on. "It'll be five years come July. I'd just gotten out of the Merchant Marine and I saw this baby lying in the sand, yip-yiping for its mama. Maybe a storm washed her in from another shore. Maybe someone killed her mama. I swear I saw tears in her eyes. I picked her up and wetted her down. Then I fed her milk from a bottle. Later I gave her ground-up fish laced with vitamins. And stones too! I fed her stones because seals need them to grind up their food.

"There was an oceanarium nearby. They studied sea mammals—porpoises and seals. I made a deal with them. I did odd jobs, and they let me keep Baby with their other seals. But Baby was still mine, and she knew it. When I called her, she jumped out of the water and came to me.

"I'd been in the circus before I joined the Merchant Marine. One day my old circus boss turns up. Not the boss we have now, the one before. He tells me he wants me back.

" 'I'm agreeable,' I say, 'but you'll have to take Baby.'

"He says, 'We don't run a water carnival. What would I do with a seal? She'd need a pool, a flat car to carry it, a ramp to sun herself, a shelter, sea salt. It would cost a fortune.'

" 'She'll be a big attraction,' I tell him. I show him how she twirls a ball on her nose, dives down in the pool to bring up things you throw in, and how she does a water dance—graceful as a ballerina—down and over, down and over. He wanted me to come back, so he took the both of us."

Tomas's voice grew anxious. "The new boss says Baby don't earn her keep. He says he'll get rid of her, but so far it's only talk."

Tomas looked lovingly at his two-hundred-twenty-pound Baby, sunning herself on the ramp.

"You did a *mitzvah*," K'tonton assured him. "Baby was an orphan when you found her. Being kind to an orphan is a big *mitzvah*."

Tomas didn't know what a *mitzvah* was, but the look in K'tonton's eyes told him it was something good.

A DOUBT ENTERS K'TONTON'S HEAD

Almost two weeks had passed since the man on the white horse brought K'tonton to the circus. K'tonton now had his own room in the camper. Papa Joe curtained off a small space on a shelf near Lillibelle's bunk, and Mama Belle furnished it. There was a bed, which Lillibelle made out of a candy box. Near the bed stood a small washstand with a tiny china bowl and water pitcher on top. Daisy bought it for him in a store that sells furniture for dollhouses.

As soon as K'tonton got out of bed in the morning, he washed his hands and recited his prayers. One prayer was really a reminder: "Listen my son, to the teaching of your father, and do not forget what your mother has taught you." When K'tonton came to this verse, he always added a prayer of his own: "Please God, send Elijah back soon with my father and mother."

K'tonton still believed that the man on the white horse

was Elijah. It did not enter his head that he might have made a mistake—until the day he visited Clown Alley.

Clown Alley wasn't a real alley. It was a tent where the clowns practiced their tricks and got ready for the show. K'tonton's friend Clarence brought him there. K'tonton sat on a table to watch Clarence put on his makeup. First the clown covered his hair with a cotton cap. Then he powdered his face and made it all white. Then he rubbed his nose with cold cream and pasted on a comical nose made of putty.

Clarence was painting on a big smile when K'tonton saw something that made him jump up in excitement. A clown they called the Professor was juggling lighted torches.

"That's what Simeon ben Gamaliel used to do," K'tonton cried out. His voice was small, but it carried a long way. The Professor stopped juggling.

"Where did you see this Simeon?" he asked. "I thought I had a *new* routine."

"I didn't see him. Simeon lived long before I was born. Simeon lived in Jerusalem when the Holy Temple was still there. That was maybe two thousand years ago. Simeon wasn't a juggler. He was a rabbi." And K'tonton told them about the Celebration of the Drawing of the Water, which comes during the holiday of Sukkot, the day Simeon ben Gamaliel did his juggling. All the clowns gathered around to listen.

"In the Land of Israel," K'tonton said, "it rains only in the winter. If the rains don't come, they have no water. They don't have food either, because the fields dry up. So on this holiday—we call it *Simḥat Bet ha-Sho'evah*, the Cele-

bration of the Drawing of the Water—they prayed for rain.

"The *Kohanim,* the priests in the temple, filled a golden pitcher with water from a brook and poured it on the altar, and everyone marched around it carrying palm branches and singing.

"But the most exciting part began the night before, outside in the Temple court. Young priests climbed up ladders and lit golden bowls filled with oil. The light was so bright, it lit up the whole city of Jerusalem. The Levites —they were the ones who helped the *Kohanim*—sang psalms and played on flutes and harps and cymbals. The people, even the rabbis, sang and danced with lighted torches. They were so thankful to God who sent the sun and rain to make things grow. For Rabbi Simeon, lighting just one torch wasn't enough. He lit eight torches and juggled them." K'tonton looked at the Professor. "The way *you* do," he said.

Then K'tonton told them about other rabbis who could juggle. "One juggled eight knives," he said. "Another juggled eight glasses of wine, another eight eggs, or maybe it was four eggs. I'm not sure how many eggs, but I know the eggs weren't cooked. They were raw, and if the rabbi didn't catch the eggs just right, they would break."

"I like those rabbis," the Professor said. "Tell me more about them."

So K'tonton told them the story of Torah on One Leg.

"This is about two rabbis," K'tonton began, "Hillel and Shammai. Both rabbis loved God and the Torah. Hillel was gentle and patient, but Shammai was very stern.

"A man came to Shammai's house and said, 'Teach me

your Torah, but teach it to me quickly, while I stand on one leg.'

"The Torah is God's law. Shammai had spent his whole life studying it. And here was a man asking him to teach it all in a few minutes! Shammai was angry. He picked up a stick and drove the man away.

"Then the man went to Hillel and said the same thing: 'Teach me the Torah while I stand on one leg.' Hillel didn't chase him away. He said, 'Listen carefully. Do not do to another person what you would not want him to do to you. This is the whole Torah. The rest is explanation.'"

The clowns applauded and said what a good storyteller K'tonton was. Clarence was so pleased, he had a *real* smile under his painted smile. But K'tonton didn't smile. He had remembered that Hillel had said something more to the man. Hillel had said, "Go now and study!"

Every day when K'tonton was home he had studied Torah with his father. That was why he knew so many stories and Bible verses. Suddenly a terrible feeling of home-sickness came over him.

That night K'tonton lay in his little bed, unable to sleep. It was an elegant bed. Lillibelle had made it out of the cover of a candy box she had saved from Valentine's Day. It was heart-shaped and had red plush sides. Daisy gave her two handkerchiefs for sheets. For a pillow, her mama made her a little silk bag filled with sweet-smelling lavender. Lillibelle herself crocheted a small, woolen afghan for a cover. Layers of cotton under the sheets made the bed soft and comfortable. But K'tonton would rather have been in his plain little bed near his mother and father.

"Why is it taking Elijah so long to come?" he wondered. "On Passover he visits every *seder* in one night."

It was then that the troubling thought came to him. "Maybe I made a mistake. Maybe the man on the white horse wasn't Elijah."

K'tonton pushed the thought away. "I must be patient," he told himself.

He began singing, very softly, a song about the *Mashiach* that he had learned at home: "Though he delay, yet I will wait for him."

Over and over K'tonton sang it until he sang himself to sleep.

MORE HAPPENINGS, BOTH GOOD AND BAD

Once the thought entered K'tonton's mind that he might have made a mistake, it kept coming back. But each time some new excitement pushed it aside.

It began on the day after his sleepless night. K'tonton was standing on Papa Joe's shoulder, watching the performers enter the Big Top. The riders on their palomino horses set him thinking about Elijah. Could he be sure the man on the white horse was Elijah? Then Jumbo came by with Lillibelle on his back. Perched on Lillibelle's shoulders was her little monkey, George. They were passing into the arena when George reached out, picked K'tonton up in his long fingers, and set him down on his own back. It was too late for Papa Joe to interfere. Circus people never interrupt a show.

"Don't worry, K'tonton," Lillibelle whispered. "We're just going around the ring. Papa will take you back on our way out."

K'tonton wasn't worried. He was having a grand time. The band was playing. Bareback riders, standing on their horse's backs, smiled and threw kisses. Funny clowns ran in and out. The people in the stands, especially the children, laughed and pointed.

"I'm a performer," K'tonton thought, "and not in the sideshow. I'm in the Big Top."

Around the ring they paraded, almost to the exit. Suddenly George leaped from Lillibelle's shoulders and landed on a trampoline in the ring. K'tonton grabbed hold of the monkey's jacket and held on tight. Up and down, up and down George jumped. Each jump was higher than the one before.

George reached the tightrope and pulled himself up. Carefully he made his way across, balancing himself with his tail. A spotlight followed him. Now he was on a rope ladder, climbing up.

From the bottom of the ladder, Lillibelle called to him to come down, but George climbed to the very top. A flying leap through the air and he was on the trapeze, swinging high.

The band had stopped playing. Far below, the people, performers and spectators, were looking up. From where K'tonton was swinging, they all looked like K'tontons.

"I'm not afraid," K'tonton told himself. "A performer is never afraid."

But he *was* afraid, so afraid he could not even recite the *Shema*. The words of the prayer stuck in his throat. He shut his eyes. A rush of air told him they were again swinging through space. When he opened his eyes, George was back on the rope ladder, going down. Lillibelle was climbing up to meet them. She grabbed George in her arms.

"Are you all right, K'tonton?" she asked.

The drums in the band rolled. The spectators stood up, clapped, and cheered. They liked the act. They thought it was part of the show.

But Papa Joe didn't like it. "The monkey must go," he said when he came into the camper that night. "We can't have such goings on." His voice was stern.

"But Papa," Lillibelle held the little monkey tight. "George didn't mean to be naughty. He was trying to be like Curious George in my book. This morning I saw him looking at the pictures."

Papa Joe smiled, then looked stern again. "It makes no difference what he meant. It's what he did. He upset the timing. He gave the high-wire performers the jitters. He might have put the gear out of line. If he had, do you know what could have happened to your mama?"

As K'tonton listened anxiously, he thought of the little stray kitten he had hurt once without meaning to. He had asked for forgiveness on Yom Kippur. He also had asked the kitten to forgive him. The little monkey looked sorry. K'tonton hoped that *he* would be forgiven.

Mama Belle was speaking. "Couldn't we give George one more chance?"

Papa Joe looked at Lillibelle. Her eyes were begging him to listen to Mama. "All right," he said. "We'll give him one more chance. But he's not to come near the Big Top again."

"He won't. I promise. I'll lock him up when I go out."

The next thing that kept K'tonton's mind off his mistake was the benefit performance.

"A benefit," Daisy explained, "is when people pay a circus to come to their town. Then they sell tickets and the money goes to a charity."

This benefit was to help a hospital for crippled children. The patients were brought to the circus and stopped at the sideshow on their way to the Big Top. There were boys and girls with casts and braces and crutches and walkers. A few were in wheelchairs.

K'tonton didn't just sit in his chair and autograph his pictures. He autographed two casts, one on a boy's leg and one on a little girl's arm. He stood on his head, walked on his hands, and turned somersaults and cartwheels. He even did a double flip backward.

The children laughed and begged for more.

"They loved it, K'tonton," Lillibelle said after the children had left. "You're a regular clown."

"Clarence taught me," K'tonton told her.

"Lillibelle," he said, "all the children didn't come. Two of them had to stay in bed. I heard the nurse say so."

Then he told her how once on the holiday of Purim he had hidden in a plate of cakes and candies and surprised a sick little boy.

"David—he's my friend now—was very sad," K'tonton said. "He'd been sick and in bed for a long time, but I made him laugh and laugh. Lillibelle, couldn't you and I go to the hospital to give those children a show? We'd get back before the big performance is over. George and Chichi could do their tricks and I could be the clown."

Lillibelle liked the idea. "But we won't take George," she said, "just Chichi. George might get into trouble again."

K'tonton didn't have a clown suit, but he put on pajamas, and Lillibelle found a piece of ribbon in her mama's sewing basket and made ruffles for his ankles and neck. She also made him a paper clown hat. Then she put on her sparkly dress, threw a cape over it, dressed Chichi in his little red jacket, and they started out. K'tonton rode in her handbag. She left it a little open at the top for air to get in.

No one in the hospital saw them as they tiptoed through the halls and peeked into the rooms. In one room, two little boys were on opposite beds.

"We're from the circus," Lillibelle told them. She threw off her cape and danced and sang for them. She made Chichi walk on his hind legs and count.

"One!" Lillibelle said. Chichi gave one bark.

"Two!" Lillibelle said. Chichi barked twice.

"Three!" Chichi gave three barks.

They counted to five.

Then, "Katchoo! Katchoo!" Lillibelle pretended to sneeze.

"Excuse me," she said, "I must get my handkerchief."

She put her hand into her bag and took out—not a handkerchief, but K'tonton! The boys stared wide-eyed. They laughed and clapped their hands. K'tonton did every trick he knew.

"We have to go now," Lillibelle said after they had been there awhile. She put K'tonton back into her bag, blew kisses to the boys, and picked up Chichi.

They left through one door as a nurse and doctor entered through another. From the hall they could hear the boys talking excitedly about a beautiful circus girl, her dog, and a tiny boy who did tricks for them.

"There's been so much talk about the circus," the nurse said to the doctor, "the children must have dreamed about it. It's strange, though, that both of them should have had the same dream."

Out in the hall Lillibelle and K'tonton giggled.

The other thing that took K'tonton's mind off his worries was cotton candy. He didn't eat it. A little girl dropped some right on top of his head. She had not meant to do it. Her father had lifted her up to watch K'tonton autograph a picture, and it slipped out of her hands. The more K'tonton tried to get the candy off, the more tangled he became. It covered his hands, his shirt, his face. It got into his hair.

"Hi, sweetie!" someone called, "You look good enough to eat."

K'tonton didn't think that was funny.

Luckily, cotton candy is made of spun sugar, which melts in hot water. Lillibelle and her mama were able to wash it out.

"This was bad, but not *so* bad," Mama Belle said as she handed K'tonton a clean shirt. "I hope nothing worse ever happens to you."

But something worse did happen to K'tonton, the very next day.

THE MAN ON THE WHITE HORSE RETURNS

It was early in the morning. Lillibelle and K'tonton were alone under the Big Top. She was teaching him to ride bareback, not on a palomino horse but on Chichi, her little dog! Chichi was running fast and K'tonton was standing on his back when he happened to look up. Coming toward him was the man on the white horse. K'tonton almost tumbled into the sawdust.

"Hello!" said the tall man. "If it isn't the little tyke."

"Did you bring them?" K'tonton asked.

"Bring who?"

"My mother and father—to take us to Jerusalem."

"Jerusalem? The Big Boss didn't say anything about taking the circus to Jerusalem."

"But Elijah is supposed to take the Jews to Jerusalem," K'tonton insisted. "To meet the *Mashiach.*" The old doubt entered his mind. "You *are* Elijah the Prophet, aren't you?" he asked.

"A prophet! Me a prophet?" The man laughed out loud. "I'm no prophet."

"You've made a mistake, K'tonton," Lillibelle said gently. "This is Mark. When we come to a new place, he rides into town to advertise the show. He's been off for a while, so you haven't seen him."

K'tonton slid off the dog's back and ran. He didn't want to see anyone or talk to anyone. He wanted to be alone.

"K'tonton, wait for me! K'tonton!" Lillibelle was following him.

K'tonton ran under a circus wagon to hide. Lillibelle's voice died away. Now K'tonton heard another sound, a deep sigh. Someone else was under the wagon, lying face down. It was Clarence, the clown.

K'tonton forgot his own troubles. "Clarence!" he called.

The clown rolled over. "The little one!" he said.

"Is something wrong?" K'tonton asked anxiously.

"I'm nothing but a clown, that's what's wrong!" Clarence wasn't wearing his greasepaint, so K'tonton could see how unhappy he looked. "Doctors save lives. Carpenters build things. All I do is make people laugh. It's time I got myself a *useful* job."

"But Clarence, making people laugh is *very* useful," K'tonton assured him. "It says so in the Talmud. That's the book my father studies."

Then he told Clarence a story.

"Once, long ago, there was a rabbi. His name was Rabbi Beroka. He was walking in the market with the Prophet Elijah. Elijah knew the answer to every question, so Rabbi Beroka asked, 'Is there anyone here who surely will have a share in the world to come?' Elijah looked around.

"There were important people in the market—princes and rich merchants and scholars. But do you know who Elijah pointed to? He pointed to two clowns! He said, 'These two surely will go to heaven. They cause laughter that makes sad hearts glad.'"

"You mean," Clarence said, "that the clowns were more important than all those princes and scholars?"

"That's what Elijah said."

Clarence pressed K'tonton's tiny hand to his heart. "K'tonton," he said, "you have made this sad heart glad." And he smiled.

But K'tonton's heart was not glad. That night he lay in his little bed, unable to sleep. Thoughts kept running around and around in his head. It was as if two K'tontons were inside him, each arguing with the other.

The first K'tonton said, "How could you make such a dreadful mistake? The nations aren't turning their swords into farm tools, the way you thought. And father and mother! Nobody is bringing them. You must get up and write to tell them what has happened."

The other K'tonton inside him answered, "I can't. I'm too ashamed. Father always calls me his little wise one. What will he think when he hears that I thought a plain circus man was Elijah?"

"You must write, even if you are ashamed," the first K'tonton insisted. "Think how worried Father and Mother must be!"

At that moment the clock struck twelve.

"It's too late now," K'tonton said. "I'll write tomorrow."

But the next day he had another excuse. "There's no use writing," he told himself. "I can't tell Father where I am because the circus is always moving. Elijah could find me without an address, but Father can't."

But K'tonton knew that he must write, if only to tell his parents that he was safe.

Writing the letter wasn't easy. K'tonton began one

letter, then tore it up. He began another and tore it up, too. This is the letter he finally sent:

Dear Father and Mother,
    Do not worry about me. I am well and hope you are the same. Father, I could not wait for you in the synagogue because I made a mistake. I will tell you about the mistake when I see you. Now I am learning things about God's creatures that I did not know before. Many times I say the blessing, "Who made such as these in Thy world."
    Please Mother, do not worry about me. Many people are taking care of me. One is very, very wide, but she is kind. She even bought me kosher dishes.
    I cannot send you my address because we move to many places, but soon we will stay in one place and I will write and tell you. I miss you very much.
        From me, your loving son,
        K'tonton.

Lillibelle stamped and mailed the letter.

HANUKKAH IS COMING

The circus was moving southward. Soon it would be in its winter quarters in central Florida. K'tonton had been homesick since the day he learned that the man on the white horse was not Elijah. Now he had another reason for being homesick. Hanukkah was coming!

K'tonton had no Hebrew calendar, so each day he made a mark on a thin roll of paper. He had arrived on the first day of Kislev. Now there were twenty marks, so he knew that in five days Hanukkah would begin. What made K'tonton especially lonely was seeing everyone around him getting ready for Christmas. This year Christmas would not begin until after Hanukkah, but his friends were already busy shopping for presents, mailing Christmas cards, and talking about parties and reunions and going home. Christmas was a happy time for his friends, but it was *their* holiday, not *his*.

K'tonton thought, "If only I hadn't made my dreadful

mistake, I'd be home. Now Hanukkah is coming and I won't have anyone to celebrate with. I won't have my father and mother. I won't have Hanukkah lights or presents or *latkes* or a *dreidel*. I won't have anything." The thought made him so sad that the corners of his mouth turned down.

"Something is wrong with K'tonton," Daisy said anxiously. "He's forgotten how to smile."

"When he's not happy, neither am I," said the Human Skeleton, and the Sword Swallower agreed. Even the Wild Man of Borneo looked worried. He really wasn't as wild as he pretended to be.

"I've worried my father and mother. Now I'm worrying all my friends. I'm spoiling their holiday," K'tonton thought. "I *have* to smile."

He tried to smile. He even tried in front of a mirror. But it's hard to smile when you don't feel like smiling. K'tonton just couldn't do it.

Suddenly an idea came to him. He hurried over to his friend the clown. Chichi, the chihuahua, gave him a lift.

"Clarence," he said, "will you paint a smile on my face like the one you paint on yours when you're going into the ring?"

"Paint a smile on your face! Why?" Clarence asked. "You have a beautiful smile of your own, though I haven't seen it lately," he admitted. "We're friends, K'tonton, aren't we? Can't you tell a friend what's bothering you?"

So K'tonton told him the whole story—how his holiday was coming and he was far away from home.

"We call it Hanukkah," he explained. "We're supposed to have lights and say blessings. And we get presents and spin tops and eat *latkes*—that's a kind of pancake. My mother used to make me special tiny ones."

"Lights did you say? Like on a Christmas tree?" Clarence asked.

"No, not electric ones! These are little candles, eight for eight nights," said K'tonton. "We don't light eight of them every night. Just one on the first night, then two, then three, until there are eight. There's an extra candle to light them with. We call it a *shammash.* "

"This is very interesting," Clarence said. "Tell me more about your holiday. I've heard the name, but I don't know much about it."

So K'tonton told Clarence about the beautiful Temple, which stood in Jerusalem in the time of the Bible, almost two thousand years ago. And K'tonton told him about the light that was kept always burning—until the wicked King Antiochus marched into the Temple with a great army and put the light out.

"He wanted the Jews to give up their religion," K'tonton explained, "but Judah Maccabee and his brothers said, 'We'll fight this Syrian king and take back our Temple. We are few and they are many, but we will fight for our homes and for our Torah, our holy laws.'"

"Who won?" Clarence asked.

"Judah Maccabee did, of course," said K'tonton. "He was as brave as a lion. King Antiochus had thousands and thousands of soldiers, footmen and horsemen. He even had fighting elephants. One of the elephants trampled one of Judah's brothers. But the Jews won. Judah Maccabee's small band beat three whole armies. They took back the Temple and cleaned it.

"Then they lit the light again. That's when the miracle happened."

"What miracle?" Clarence asked.

"The miracle the *dreidel* tells about. It says *Nes gadol haya sham*—A great miracle happened there!"

"Whoa, K'tonton," Clarence interrupted, "You're going too fast for me. What is a *dreidel*?"

"It's a top with four sides," K'tonton explained. "You spin it on Hanukkah. There's a Hebrew letter on each side."

Then he told Clarence about the miracle of the oil. He explained that in the Temple the priests used a special pure kind of oil for the lamps. The oil was kept in jars stamped with the seal of the high priest. But when they returned to the Temple, all they could find was one small jarful.

"It was just enough to burn one day," K'tonton said, "but a miracle happened and it burned *eight* days, until more oil could be prepared."

"So now," K'tonton ended the story, "we light lights for eight nights and we spin *dreidels.*"

"Hmm," Clarence said, "could you show me what those Hebrew letters look like?"

He handed K'tonton four little pieces of paper to write on. K'tonton took out the bit of lead he carried in his pocket and carefully formed a *nun,* a *gimel,* a *heh,* and a *shin,* one

נ   ג   ה   ש

letter on each piece of paper.

K'tonton felt a little better when he returned to the tent. He could even smile when he tried. He was so busy trying during the next few days that he didn't notice the whispering going on around him. Clarence whispered to Daisy, and Daisy whispered to John. John whispered to the Wild Man and the Sword Swallower. Clarence, Lillibelle, her mama and papa, Tomas the animal trainer, and the flapjack man were whispering, too, and hiding packages.

Then came the first night of Hanukkah.

The circus had arrived in its winter quarters. There were no more performances, but some of the tents were up. K'tonton stood alone in one of the tents. He was looking sadly at the window, thinking of the Hanukkah light that should have been burning there. Suddenly he heard voices.

"Happy Hanukkah, K'tonton! Happy holiday!"

All of his friends were crowded into the tent. Even Jumbo the elephant stood in the doorway. Before K'tonton had time to think, Jumbo picked him up in his trunk and put him down on the windowsill.

Clarence set a little clay lamp with nine holes in it beside him. Lillibelle handed him a box of tiny candles left over from her birthday cake.

"Time for your Hanukkah light, K'tonton," Clarence said. "I'll help you light. What did you call the servant candle? Oh, yes, the *shammash*!"

There wasn't a sound in the room as K'tonton kindled the first light, reciting the blessings. His voice rose sweet and clear.

"Now tell the story," said Clarence.

So K'tonton told them the Hanukkah story just as he had told it to Clarence, except the part about the fighting elephants. He left that part out on account of Jumbo. "It isn't Jumbo's fault that his ancestors trampled Judah Maccabee's brother," K'tonton thought. "I wouldn't want to hurt his feelings."

After this, each one gave K'tonton a present and wished him a happy Hanukkah. Not all of them pronounced Hanukkah correctly. Some called it *Tsh*anukkah or *K*anukkah. But everybody got the "Happy" right.

"Thank you! *Todah! Todah rabbah!*" K'tonton said over and over again. He was so excited that he forgot his friends couldn't understand Hebrew.

Then it was time for refreshments. The flapjack man, in a high chef's hat and a white apron, served pancakes for everyone—but not the usual kind of pancakes. These were *latkes,* potato pancakes. He made some special tiny ones for K'tonton in a new doll's frying pan. Lillibelle had brought it to him as a Hanukkah present.

Daisy was on her eighteenth pancake when they heard a splash in the pool next door and then the sound of flapping flippers. Sylvia Seal flopped into the room.

"I forgot to tell you," Clarence said to the astonished K'tonton, "Sylvia wants to play *dreidel* with you."

"But we haven't any *dreidel,*" K'tonton reminded him.

"Yes we have," said Clarence.

He took out of his pocket four little pieces of paper, the ones with the Hebrew letters that K'tonton had made for him. The *nun* he pinned to the front of K'tonton's shirt, the *gimel* to the side, the *heh* to the back, and the *shin* to the other side. (Clarence used tiny safety pins so as not to stick him.)

Then Clarence picked up K'tonton and set him on Sylvia's nose. The seal pointed her nose upward and spun K'tonton around.

"I'm a *dreidel!* I'm my own *dreidel!*" K'tonton cried out while everyone watched and cheered.

Around and around K'tonton spun on Sylvia Seal's nose, until he tumbled laughing into the clown's hand.

"Want me to paint a smile on you?" Clarence asked.

"There isn't any room," K'tonton answered. And he was right. His smile was so wide, it covered his face.

THE MORNING AFTER

It was hard to believe. Less than a day had passed since the Hanukkah party, and K'tonton's smile was gone again.

"Didn't you like the party?" Clarence asked.

"It was a wonderful party," K'tonton told him.

"Then why are you so sad?" Clarence asked.

K'tonton didn't answer. His feelings were hard to explain. Before the party he had thought mostly of himself, how lonely he would be on Hanukkah without his parents. Now he kept thinking about his parents, how lonely they must feel without him. He wondered whether they had received his letter.

"Are you homesick?" Clarence asked.

K'tonton nodded.

"Would you like to go home?"

K'tonton looked troubled. "I've been away so long, and I waited until last week to write to my father and mother. Maybe they won't want me," he said.

"They'll want you," Clarence assured him, "and I think I know a way to get you back to them quickly. Not that I like helping you leave us, but parents come first."

"Hop into my pocket," he said. "I'll take you over to a friend who raises pigeons. There's another pigeon fancier down your aunt's way who ships my friend homers to send back. Your parents can meet you at your aunt's house."

K'tonton didn't know what pigeons had to do with getting him home, but he hopped in.

"We're here," Clarence said after they had walked awhile. K'tonton looked out. Clarence's friend was standing on the roof of a shed, exercising his pigeons. K'tonton watched with delight as they circled overhead, their wings flashing against the sky.

Clarence climbed up a ladder to his friend.

"This is the little one I told you about," he said. "K'tonton, this is Michael. Michael, this is K'tonton."

"I'm pleased to meet you," Michael said. He was a tall, young man with red hair. His warm smile made K'tonton feel welcome.

"K'tonton has a problem," Clarence said, and he told Michael about it. "I thought you might be able to send him to his aunt's by carrier pigeon."

Michael looked interested. "You're light enough," he said, weighing K'tonton in his hand. "I've sent messages that weighed more. Where did you say your aunt lives?"

"In South Carolina," K'tonton told him.

"Where in South Carolina?"

K'tonton gave him the name of the town.

"Now that's what I call luck," Michael said, looking

pleased. "Tommy lives in the same town. Tommy's this friend of mine who races homers. He ships me a bird. When I release it, it flies straight home. Here is one that just came."

Michael reached into a crate and drew out a handsome pigeon with an especially broad breast.

"This is Pete," Michael said. "He belongs to my friend Tommy. If I say so myself, our pigeons are faster than the mail. I'll send you off with Pete first thing in the morning. You won't mind flying with him, will you?"

"No," said K'tonton. "I've already flown with a sparrow and a yellow bird, even a gull."

"Good! You'll stay here overnight. I'll send you off first thing in the morning."

"Can't I say good-bye to my friends? Can't I thank them?" pleaded K'tonton.

"Better not!" This time it was Clarence who spoke. "If the Big Boss knows you're leaving, he may make trouble. He considers you a valuable property."

"But Clarence, won't Papa Joe get into trouble? He's supposed to take care of me."

"Don't worry about Papa Joe," Clarence answered. "He'll be glad you're back with your own papa and mama. So will all your friends. I'll say good-bye for you, but not until you're safely on your way."

The sun had just risen when Clarence returned next morning. K'tonton and Pete the pigeon were standing on a table. They already had become friends. Pete held his head high and proud, not bobbing like the pigeons K'tonton saw in city parks.

Mike had cut narrow strips out of an old woolen muffler and wound them around K'tonton. He would have looked like a tiny Egyptian mummy, except that his face showed and his arms and legs were free.

"I meant to line your jacket with newspaper," Clarence told K'tonton. "Newspaper is good for keeping out the cold. It can get pretty cold up there. But the wool is a better idea. Now, here's some lunch for the trip."

He tucked two tiny sandwiches and a few pill-sized capsules of water between the woolen strips. Mike inserted a note into a small plastic container and attached it to a ring on one of Pete's legs.

"It looks like a clear day ahead, and the wind is right," Mike told Clarence. "They'll probably make it to Tom's place before nightfall." He bound K'tonton firmly on Pete's back. Then he released the pigeon into the air.

"Good-bye, good-bye! Have a good trip!" Clarence called. Pete flew straight up and then turned north. K'tonton was on his way.

IN THE MEANTIME

Perhaps you are wondering whether K'tonton's parents received his letter. It reached them on the first day of Hanukkah. A postal strike had delayed the delivery.

For more than three weeks, K'tonton's mother kept saying to his father, "How could you leave the child on a windowsill? Maybe he fell off and broke an arm or a leg."

Over and over again his father answered, "It was only for a few minutes. If he fell off, I'd have found him. I searched all over the synagogue, near the window, under the benches, in the ark. I even looked outside on the lawn and sidewalk."

Both parents kept reminding each other that K'tonton often disappeared. It is easy for a thumb-sized child to get lost. Each time he had returned safely. But how could they be sure he would return this time?

Now they knew from the letter that their little son was

alive and well. But why hadn't he told them what his mistake was? More important, where was he now?

Again K'tonton's parents read the letter, searching for clues. "Many times I say the blessing, 'Who made such as these in Thy world.'" This was the blessing recited when one saw a beautiful animal for the first time. Where could K'tonton be seeing beautiful animals? On a farm? In a zoo? But farms and zoos don't move from place to place. They stay put.

A circus!

K'tonton's father and mother came up with the answer at the same time. A circus has all kinds of animals, the most beautiful in the world. And there was that friend K'tonton had mentioned who was "very, very wide." Could he have meant the Fat Lady? K'tonton would be too polite to call her fat.

"We must find out whether a circus was near your sister's town when K'tonton disappeared," his father said. "We'll take the bus to South Carolina first thing tomorrow morning."

So it happened that, as K'tonton was flying to his aunt's town by pigeon, his parents were traveling there by bus.

TOGETHER AT LAST

K'tonton's parents and his widowed aunt stood near the window, lighting the candles for the third night of Hanukkah. They didn't feel like celebrating. They had not yet found K'tonton. But one must kindle lights on Hanukkah, so they did. K'tonton's father had just recited the second blessing, thanking God "who worked miracles for our fathers in days of old," when he heard a faint "Amen."

"I'm imagining things," he thought. "I've longed so much for K'tonton that now I think I hear him."

A tapping on the windowpane made him look out. A young man was standing outside the window carrying a pigeon in his hands. Seated on the pigeon's back was K'tonton.

In a minute the window went up, and K'tonton was in his father's hands. Later, after Tommy had come inside, K'tonton's father said to him, "Now I know how Noah must have felt when the dove returned to the ark with an olive leaf in its beak."

"It's a *nes,* another miracle!" his aunt cried.

"A *nes,*" his mother repeated. She pressed her tiny son to her cheek. She removed the woolen bands that Mike had wound about him. She dropped eighteen silver coins into the charity box and whispered her thanks to God. Then she seated K'tonton in a tiny chair before a little table that stood on the kitchen table.

"You'll talk later. Eat now. You must be starved," K'tonton's mother insisted.

She hurried into the kitchen and soon returned with a stack of tiny potato pancakes. She made them by dropping

tiny bits of batter into the hot oil and then quickly lifting them out again. It took less than a minute.

K'tonton's aunt served Pete a bowl of *nahit* (chick peas) and Tommy a big stack of regular-sized pancakes.

Then, at last, K'tonton told his story. It wasn't easy. When he tried to explain why he had waited so long to write, he hung his head, ashamed. But his father put a finger under his chin and lifted it.

"Older and even wiser people than you have made bigger mistakes," he said. "You will know better next time." His father smiled. "Have you forgotten that one is supposed to rejoice on this holiday? Your mother and I are filled with joy to have you back. You must be joyful, too."

Then K'tonton's father sat down and wrote a note for Pete to carry with him when Tommy sent him back. It was full of blessings and thanks to Mike, Clarence, and all the circus friends who had been kind to his little son. He had to write very small to get it all in.

Two days later, on Shabbat Hanukkah, K'tonton was again in the synagogue, the same synagogue from which he had disappeared almost a month before. Standing before the congregation, high up on the stand where the Torah is read, K'tonton thanked God "who is kind even when we don't deserve it" and who had brought him safely home.

The people in the congregation, who had been praying every day for his return, responded, "May He who showed kindness to you in the past be kind to you always."

YEARS LATER

Many years have passed since the Hanukkah night that K'tonton spent in the circus.

Clarence is now an old man, but he is still a clown. Grease covers his wrinkles and a wig covers his gray hair. "Why should I retire?" he asks. "I like to make children laugh and sad hearts glad."

Lillibelle is a famous aerialist, a star in a large, three-ring circus that performs in armories and convention halls. Mama Belle and Papa Joe are very proud of her.

Papa Joe is an old man now, but he is not ready to retire. He's planning to start a small tent circus of his own, the one-ring kind. He says that the new circuses are fine for big cities, but little towns need entertainment, too. His circus will be much like the one K'tonton was in, but with one exception: it won't have a sideshow.

Daisy and John both have retired. Each lives in a little

cottage in the town where they spent so many winters while they were in the circus. Daisy sits on her porch afternoons, and the children coming home from school stop and visit with her. She tells them stories about her life in the circus. Their favorite stories are about K'tonton.

Daisy has tried to lose weight, but she hasn't been very successful. She is always giving the children treats, and before she knows it, a peanut or a candy is in her mouth or she is licking a lollipop or an ice-cream cone.

John is still very thin, but he is no longer a human skeleton. He enjoys eating all the fattening foods he used only to dream about.

Tomas and Sylvia have left the circus and are in a place called The Institute for Oceanographic Research. Tomas thought that Baby might be happier with other seals. "Besides," he said, "it will be a *mitzvah* for her to help the scientists in their research. They are studying seals and porpoises to find a cure for the bends."

K'tonton and his parents live in a kibbutz in Israel. Sometimes the fig trees and the vineyards in the kibbutz remind K'tonton of the mistake he made long ago, when he thought a circus rider was Elijah.

"Father," he once asked, "when will the real Elijah and the real *Mashiach* come?"

"The *Mashiach* will come when the world is ready for him," his father answered. He opened the Hebrew Bible they were studying and pointed to a passage. It was the same passage that K'tonton had thought of when he sat under the fig tree in his aunt's garden.

Nation shall not lift up sword against nation.
Neither shall they learn war anymore;
but everyone will sit under his vine and under his fig tree
and none shall make them afraid.

"When you see this happen," K'tonton's father said, "you will know that the *Mashiach* has come. You can't hurry the *Mashiach*, K'tonton, but you *can* help make the world ready for him."

And that is just what K'tonton is doing. Every week —often several times a week—he visits hospitals to entertain the sick children there, Jewish children and Arab children.

"It's K'tonton!" they call when they see their tiny friend. "Do tricks for us, K'tonton."

And K'tonton does all the clown tricks he learned from Clarence.

The children, even the very sick ones, laugh and clap their hands. It makes K'tonton almost glad to be thumbsized.

"*Sim Shalom!*" he sings on the way home, "*Sim Shalom! Send peace!*"

About the Author

Sadie Rose Weilerstein has been a leading author of Jewish children's books and short stories for over fifty years. Among her books are *What the Moon Brought, Little New Angel, What Danny Did,* and *Ten and a Kid.* K'tonton, the best known of her characters, made his first appearance in a story published in the September 1930 issue of *Outlook* magazine. He subsequently became the hero of four books —*The Adventures of K'tonton, K'tonton in Israel, K'tonton on an Island in the Sea,* and *The Best of K'tonton.* Mrs. Weilerstein received a special Jewish Book Council Award for her "cumulative contribution to Jewish juvenile writing" and the Women's League for Conservative Judaism's Yovel Award "in recognition of her outstanding and pioneer contributions to the world of books for Jewish children." She was given the Association of Jewish Libraries' 1980 Sydney Taylor Award for her contribution to Jewish children's literature.

About the Artist

Marilyn Hirsh is the author-illustrator of over twenty books for children. Among her books are four that she illustrated in India while serving with the Peace Corps. Her many books of Jewish interest—including *Ben Goes into Business, The Rabbi and the Twenty-Nine Witches,* and *Potato Pancakes All Around*—earned for her the 1979 Sydney Taylor Award. She also was the illustrator of *The Best of K'tonton.*